2003   2003

Given
In Celebration
of
Childhood Dreams
by
Michelle Drawz

2003   2003

My earliest memories are about wanting a horse.

I grew up in a little town in New Jersey called Oakland. Every day I walked to school past a private academy whose riding arena was on the main street. Each morning and afternoon, someone was training and exercising the horses. I got to know all of the horses' names. My favorites were Secret, a black mare, and Sugar Plum, a strawberry roan. I would delay as long as I could at the arena fence until I had to go on to school, or home.

When asked, my parents would say, "No, you cannot have a horse. They are too expensive." My sister and I saved every penny of birthday money to take a lesson on the horses at the academy. For that hour we were in heaven, and talked of nothing else for days. But what to do with all that longing?

I think if I had gotten my wish for a horse, I may not have found my love for drawing. My pencil and paints became the vehicle to my life of fantasy horses. My pencil seemed fueled by the desire to be with those exquisite animals. I loved drawing the shine of their coats and learning how to make their hooves look real from every angle. Manes and tails were places to get lost in depicting the wind blowing through them. And was the horse running or rearing? Deciding what color my dream horse would be was like deciding on my favorite ice cream flavor.

I went on to art school at Pratt Institute, where I continued my daydreaming and drawing of my favorite subjects. Now I ride almost every day and study drawing and painting as much as I can. Some things do not change.

To all our horses

Special thanks to Lisa Holton, Ann Tobias, Sharon Lerner,
Jean Marzollo, and Judy Myers

First Edition   1 3 5 7 9 10 8 6 4 2   Printed in Singapore

Library of Congress Cataloging-in-Publication Data on file

ISBN 0-7868-1995-2   Visit www.hyperionchildrensbooks.com

My Pony

SUSAN JEFFERS

HYPERION BOOKS FOR CHILDREN
NEW YORK

I want a pony.

I want a pony more than anything else in the world.

When we drive in the country,

my parents stop the car whenever

we pass by a farm.

I lean against the fence and smell the horses.

It is my favorite smell.

Every time I ask my mother if we can have a pony,

she always says the same thing:

"Ponies cost too much money."

Every time I ask my father, he says,

"We have no place to keep it."

They both say, "Maybe when you are older."
But I still want a pony. I want one now.

When I am supposed to be doing my homework,

I dream of riding my pony. I call her Silver.

She has dapples and a shiny coat.

When I draw her, it is as if she comes alive.

She is so alive, I can jump on her back—and
away we go into the night sky.

We go to a wood where
the tall trees smell all piney
and the squirrels chatter at us.
We trot over a stream with clear water
and spotted stones.
We travel in moonlight, Silver and I.

I can see the tossing manes and
flickering tails of other horses.
They stand under the trees, watching us.
Silver canters toward them,
with hooves just touching the ground.

The other horses want to know

who we are.

I touch their muzzles and forelocks.

They nicker softly and push my hand.

They are gray, palomino, chestnut,

and blue roan.

All of them are beautiful, but none is

as beautiful as Silver.

No matter where I go, Silver is with me.

We gallop through the cold mountain stream.

Together we flash like a comet across the sky.

Then we come down between two clouds.

I slip off Silver's back and give her

a dream peppermint.

When my drawing of Silver is finished,

I turn out the light.

It is time to kiss my parents good night.

I will ask again for a pony, and they may say no.

But, for now, I am happy.

Silver waits just outside my window.

Always.